Daisy

by

Stephen Cosgrove

illustrated by

Diana Rice Bonin

http:www.stephencosgrove.com
e-mail: stephen@stephencosgrove.com

HERITAGE BUILDERS   3105 Locan Avenue, Clovis, California 93619

Dedicated to all my breath brothers and sisters, horses big and small. From Ginger to Pete (aka Nitter Pitter) and the smallest of them all, Flutterby. If you listen carefully on a stormy night you can hear the thunder of their hooves as they race about Heaven's Light.

Stephen

I f you followed the glitter of a moonbeam across a starlit sky, you would find a delightful place called Heaven's Light.

It was here that tiny, winged beings called Earth Angels lived.

Also in Heaven's Light lived little, winged creatures of every sort called ArkAngels. There were FlutterBears, FlutterBunnies, and most special of all, the FlutterFly Ponies.

Beyond Heaven's Light was a soft, rolling grassland called the Heather where the ponies reared and kicked in delight as they searched for a long-lost place called the Miracle Meadow.

For, you see, a long time ago, all the FlutterFly Ponies were born on the Miracle Meadow. As they grew older, they flew from the meadow to explore the many wonders in Heaven's Light.

In time, the herds of tiny, winged ponies flew farther and farther away. They flew here, explored there, and soon all the FlutterFly Ponies simply forgot where the meadow was.

All the ponies flew in herds,
but there was one little FlutterFly Pony
that loved to fly all alone. Her mane was
as yellow as a rising sun, and her coat was
spotted here and there with the outline of
spring flowers. Everyone in Heaven's Light
called her Daisy.

Like all the other ponies, Daisy's
greatest wish was to be the first to find the
Miracle Meadow. Everyday, bathed in the
golden light of morning, she would kick
her heels and begin her search.

D

aisy chased across the skies looking here, there and everywhere, but she simply couldn't find the meadow.

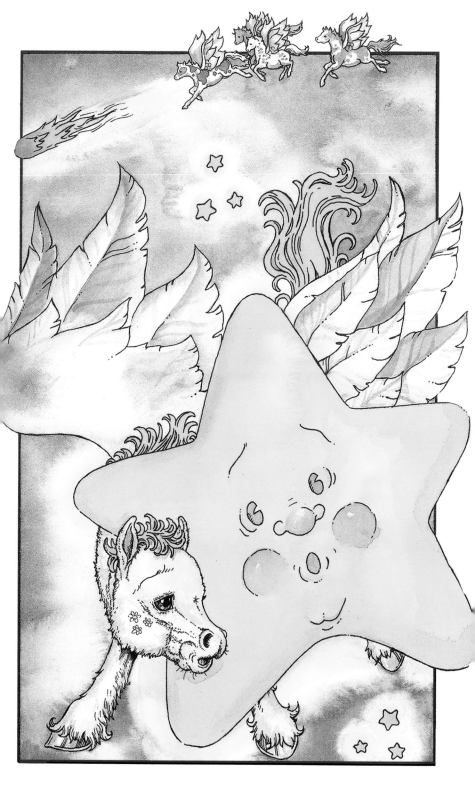

Then, one day, as Daisy sat resting on a floating cloud, she thought she saw something glowing down on the Heather. Curious, she quickly swooped below.

There she found a wonderful tiny meadow filled with sweet, purple clover growing in the deep, green grasses.

Daisy leaned down and gently plucked a single clover top from the grass. Slowly she chewed the plump, juicy blossom. It was sweeter than sweet.

This one taste was all it took.

Oh, yes! Daisy knew she had found the long-lost Miracle Meadow!

At first, Daisy was eager to tell the others about what she had found. But then she began to think, "If I tell the others they will all want to come and taste the sweet clover and grasses. There are too many FlutterFlys and not enough clover. There is only enough for a tiny taste for each, and then there won't be any for me."

Daisy selfishly decided that the Miracle Meadow would best be kept as her little secret. Carefully she pulled a big fluffy cloud over the meadow to hide it.

Safe on her meadow, Daisy began eating to her heart's content.

Suddenly, her ears perked up in warning. In the distance she could hear the flapping wings of a herd of FlutterFly Ponies flying her way.

After snatching one last bite, she lifted into the air to meet the herd before they found her secret.

She flew just as fast as she could and met them a cloud or two away. "Hi, guys," she whinnied, "what are you doing here?"

"We are looking for the Miracle Meadow," one of them answered. "What are you doing here?"

"Oh, not munch uh, much," she said, "I was just resting on the Miracle Meadow. I mean, uh nesting on a riracle fellow, er, uh..."

"So, you found it?" one of them asked slyly.

"It? It what?" innocently answered Daisy.

"The Miracle Meadow and the clover," cried out a little stallion, wings flapping in glee, "for what is that hanging from the corner of your mouth?"

Sure enough, caught in the corner of Daisy's mouth was a plump, purple clover top.

Excitedly the ponies began shouting, "Hurry! Hurry! Daisy found the Miracle Meadow!"

Quickly the skies filled with the flapping wings of a hundred ponies, all flying in Daisy's direction.

Swiftly she swooped to the ground to protect what she considered to be her Miracle Meadow.

Of course, all of the other ponies followed.

She stood in the middle of the meadow and snapped at the herd, "It's mine! I found it! It's mine!"

As could be expected, the others ignored her.

Daisy flapped from spot to spot trying to keep everyone away, but there were too many ponies and only one of her. As she blocked this way, they would zip around her tail and snap up a bite of clover.

Tiny hooves angrily stomped about.

Finally, everyone stopped and looked around. There was nothing left except trampled grass and smashed purple clover.

"Oh, well," muttered one of the ponies, "This couldn't have been the Miracle Meadow. There is nothing special here." Then one-by-one all the little FlutterFly Ponies flew away.

The only one left was Daisy, her wings drooped to the ground.

She sadly looked around at all that her greed had caused. "It was so beautiful," she sniffed, "but now it is ruined because I didn't want to share."

As Daisy cried, crystal tears of sorry dripped down her cheeks and splashed to the ground below.

"From now on," she sobbed, "I will share all that I find."

Then she slowly lifted into the sky.

As she flew away there were gentle movements on this tiny patch of crushed meadow. At each spot where Daisy's tears had fallen, tiny green shoots pushed up from the ground -- glowing shoots of the sweetest grass, and plump purple clover.

The Miracle Meadow was still alive.

Poor little Daisy flew far away
thinking the ground was bare,
but the grass grew back, green as could be
and Daisy learned how to share

More to this story at BookPop.com

BookPop Books
collect them all

Azalea

Daisy

Rosebud

Thistle

Sniffles | Number 1

Buttermilk | Number 2

Creole` | Number 3

Fanny | Number 4

Flutterby | Number 5

Leo the Lop | Number 6

Morgan & Me | Number 7

MuffinDragon | Number 8

Fiddler T. Bear

GramdPa Sam

Gabriel FaintHeart

Pretty, Pretty Prettina

www.StephenCosgrove.com